I Hide in The Rain

A Collection of Flash Fiction

Jacquinita A. Rose

Disclaimer

ISBN: 978-1-944167-19-6
ISBN: 978-1-944167-20-2 (Paperback)
Library of Congress Control Number: 2017906013

Dedication.

This collection is dedicated to all of us who tend to hide in plain sight.

Acknowledgments

A special note of thanks goes to my family, friends and to you for your continued support and encouragement of this work and of Grown Folks' Publishing.

Foreword

I Hide in the Rain is a compilation of flash fiction that expresses the highs and lows of relationships, deepest feelings about self, sentimental value of possessions from loved ones, culture, death, and so much more. It's not just a collection of stories to read and be done. These stories are intricately woven together with such imagery and drips with masterful writing that you will find yourself reading these stories over again. This collection will have you on a rollercoaster of happiness and epiphany with a touch of poetic class.

Table of Contents

I Hide in the Rain

I hide in the rain. There is no other place to be. I exist unseen. I move in unison to the drops of liquid pounding against my skin. I am invisible in plain sight. No one sees me nor tries to. Shades and tones of every type combined with shapes of every size pass quickly to their perceived destinations. Some constantly examine their toes, undisturbed by the chaos around them. Others march forward, blindly, with electronic accessories stuck to their ears like oversized earrings while sipping tongue-twisting concoctions from $8 white paper cups.

Slow large drops quicken to small fast stinging pricks. I hide even further. My vantage point a small unattended bench freshly washed to expose the rusting iron beneath.

I try to catch peace but he slides through my fingers like flour through a sieve. I want to find hope but she antici-pates my every move and eludes me at every turn. I hunt for love but her arms are already full. I desire rest but I'm too hungry for life to be ready for the grave. I am a kettle of contradictions.

My façade of perfection slips away with the last rain soaked curl of my moments-ago visit to the hair salon. My white starch shirt is now a graffiti canvas decorated with colored strips of mauve rouge, extra-volume mascara, sable foundation, and raspberry lipstick.

Yet, I hide in the rain where layers of illusions are washed away. Ineffective umbrellas broken by the weight of the truth provide no protection. There is no escape from the truth. Doubt has become one of my two lovers. I lay next to him each night. Fear, the other, cradles me to sleep. They both talk to me during my breakfast. Doubt is louder than button four on my high-powered juicer. I have given him the power to chain me to a reality not of my own making.

Change is my secret wish but I am bound by fear. The mortgage must be paid. God forbid, the three numbers that define me fall any lower! Responsible is the name I now bear. It replaces the name given to me at birth.

To do what must be done requires me to unshackle my chains. But they've become comfortable bracelets. To abide by other's expectations of me is proof of my sound judgement. Any other road taken would shine light on my presumed lack of wisdom.

I breathe to take a moment to digest the six-lane highway of thoughts speeding through my mind. The sun emerges from behind snow-white clouds. The octave-eight piano chord emanating from my purse signals my thirty minutes are over. I empty the contents of my rain soaked shoes.

I dream for the day when my time becomes my own and the pen becomes my passion. I close my eyes for a few seconds. I open them and accept today is not that day. I toss my white paper cup in the trash bin beside the bench. With a nod of my head I acknowledge the passerby with purple-laced sneakers. I wave to the young child playing in her fully-equipped stroller.

I am interrupted from my civility by the sound of piano music now radiating from my tote bag. It's time to return to open-shared office space and once a month bill-paying monotony.

But for now I take comfort in that I hide in the rain.

Don't Forget Your Jacket

"Baby Girl, don't forget your jacket!" I call to a retreating
back. My warning carries on through the wind toward
young school-bus bound ears. "I didn't, Mama," Steph-
anie says as she raises it to bear witness of her statement.
Light pink with purple-polka dots. "I love you," she
mouths through the back window as it drives away. Then
suddenly she disappears. I pause to catch my breath.
Once again I lost myself in recollections of misty day-
dreams. Thirty years have come and gone since that
day. Yet, lately it seems like it's now, right here in my
hand, where I can easily touch it. But the past plays
hide-n-seek with the soul and time ravages the mind. I
am now a guest in my own home. What was once familiar now seems strange and out of place.

Bills, letters, and packages left by the postman, ad-
dressed to someone else's name, sit in my wicker basket
next to the table by the front door. Now, the tables are
reversed. My mind does not quite catch up to the words
from my mouth. Memory once sharp as the blade of the
military man's sword now is too dull to slice softened

butter. I attempt games of 'remember when' through the playground of my thoughts. I hide but do not recall what it is that I seek.

The wind races through blankets of red, gold, and auburn leaves. The bird's breath is like little puffs of smoke. A hint of familiarity stirs. My toes ache for the feel of dew covered grass. The Sun calls to me through floor-to-ceiling clear-pane glass windows. I rise from my chair, to walk to my room. There is something there that I need. But before me lies a hall of fresh waxed hardwood floors with faint smells of pine disinfectant.

I turn to my right. Pictures, reflections of a long-lived life, staring back at me adorn lilac colored walls. Memories from a distant past bring glimpses of overabundant love. Strangers call to me as though they know me. Soothing words from unrecognizable faces.

A soft touch to my shoulder brings waves of comfort. "Mama, don't forget your jacket."

The Right Side of Happy

James and I failed as lovers. Yet, in spite of every other weekend visits, split holidays, and parking lot car-seat exchanges, we excelled as friends.

The double folded, foiled pressed mint 100% recycled paper in my hand, a reflection of an obligated request. Why did I accept? A well-timed illness suited the situation.

Too late. I'm welcomed at the door by a familiar deep baritone with Southern-charm manners, smooth mocha skin, and marshmallow-white hair.

"Good afternoon, Ma'am." A bow of the head points me to the courtyard outside. I remember the way. Seconds later my path is blocked by a herd of hormones gathered to mingle and sample wealth not their own.

"How are you?" The standard question asked in an octave too high. Their reward, "I'm fine, thank you" delivered with perfect pitch. A borage of time-wasted rambles bore me. An escaped yawn conveys my feigned interest. They scatter to find another prey.

From, the safety of the second floor balcony window, she attempts to pierce me with a glare to ensure I keep my word and forever hold my peace. Doubt simmers beneath the surface. A painted-on curtain length dress, extra-hold hairspray, French-tip manicured nails, and 48-hour colon cleanse, complete her façade of perfection.

The father of my children trusts me, yet another thinks he's blind. Strange are the behaviors of those in the present who fear the power of the past. The soon-to-be *mrs* understands what he cannot. Love hides behind a veil of friendship. Though no need for her to worry. I'm a fool to reveal myself now. The years are gone. The twins are the only evidence of a shared lifetime. No words can recapture what he doesn't miss.

The games begin with the exchange of vows and finish with the jumping of a broom. Now joined by God, her lungs deflate and she breathes a sigh of relief. Deceitful eyes extend to me no expressions of thankfulness, only smug uncertainty. Dismissing the fact that the prospect of her future moments ago lay in the silence of my voice.

For the first dance, James serenades her with the Tennessee Waltz. Not quite what I expected. She stumbles during the dip, so we clap to reassure her. The third change in clothing brings no improvement to her disposition; waist-slimming pantyhose can't eliminate insecurity.

Satisfied from her fill of lobster, shrimp, blue-cheese crumbles atop filet mignon, and a miniscule sip of wine, she rises like a queen prepared to welcome her subjects. Raised glasses of faux chardonnay followed by sarcastic curtsies build false confidence.

Butterfly kisses on the cheek of the man to the left are tender moments staged for the benefit of the guests, ignorant of their part in her scheme. Reciprocated squeezes hint at promises of later delights. Though consummation depends on the well-timed potency of one blue pill.

Diamond engraved cuffs, a starched collar, and grey-hair dye do wonders for a man. Perhaps I shouldn't have told

him to get out. Years ago I ended up leaving. Why?
Pride; a stupid thing which gave me confidence to believe
I made the best decision.

Now here I stand, reliving a time when I was brand new
like her. But I danced to the thud of the morning paper,
made love to a husband who put out the trash, and
owned a lawn which passed inspection of the Homeown-
ers Association.

Memories serve to entice us. One day, I'll reach a place
when I won't remember the number of years, months,
days, hours, minutes, or seconds since I last wore his
name. Until then, for the children's sake or my own, I
suppress my disappointment and regret to congratulate
her; the one who took my place on the right side of happy.

A Day Like Today

I'm John Jackson III, husband, friend, and brother.
There are four of us including me. I am second after
Jacob, then comes Brian and Sally. Family means everything to me. I want us all to spend more time together as
a family. You know, continue old traditions and start
some new ones. I'm the one who coordinates the family
get-togethers. I don't mind. I plan family events at least
once a month to try to get us all to gather in one place.
It's not easy, but I try. I didn't plan this get together, but
I'm happy everyone was able to attend.

—

I see my wife, Jill and my Mom admiring my appearance.
I don't say anything.

"I think John looks good in this tie," Jill says admiring
the gold and blue stripes. I should have been honest with
her. I don't like those stripes. I prefer solid colors. I
wore that tie for years to please Jill, because it makes her
smile. Although, she hasn't smiled much lately. Her eyes

look so tired. Jill's too beautiful of a woman for that. I wish I could dry her eyes.

"John loves those slacks." Mom's right. But I never told Jill why I loved those slacks. Those blue slacks minimize the size of my waist and make the pleats more pronounced. I wore those same blue slacks at least three times a week.

My mom and Jill seem to disagree about almost everything except the fact they both love me. Now, both picked out my clothes together. I am handsome, with my starched white gloves, and my tamed sideburns. For 15 years I prayed for the day, Mom and Jill would agree on something related to me. I guess my prayers were answered on a day like today.

Oh, there's my baby brother Brian and his wife, Janet. Their schedules were too hectic to come to Thanksgiving Dinner. Jill had gone all out with the turkey and all the trimmings, but I understand. Brian was up for a new promotion so he and Janet chose to spend the holiday with his boss. My sister Sally just walked in, I haven't seen her in a year. Such a shame! We had a big disagreement over the 4th of July, arguing over bun length hotdogs.

Wow, over at the front is James Reynolds, a good friend of mine, we lost touch with each other. Man, he looks fit. I didn't make it through the first week of boot camp. There would be no 21-gun salute for me. James is at least 60 years old and not a pound of body fat on him. My first entry in my calendar's "to-do" list last week was to call James today. For some reason, he'd been on my mind. If I called him now, he wouldn't answer. But I don't have to concern myself with that now.

 I just noticed my big brother Jacob, in a suit no less. Jacob is a Hawaiian shirt and flip flops kind of guy. Always jet setting off to some corner of the world. I believe he's racked up a million or more frequent flyer miles. Last year, he traveled across Europe and Asia accompanied by priceless and some unmentionable memories, no doubt. Jacob had too much jet lag and no time for the family reunion this past May. I understand. The family reunion wasn't as exotic, but it was no less interesting when Uncle Bob lost his dentures bobbing for apples. Wish Jacob had been there. Ah, but on days like today seems no one is too busy.

I'll admit I'm surprised at Jacob's presence. Last time Jacob and I spoke I wanted to get together with him for dinner, a brothers "night out." But dinner conflicted with his pending trip to Vegas. I understand. Nonrefundable tickets to Las Vegas can be expensive. Matter of fact, Jacob's flight is scheduled to leave for Las Vegas today. Mercy, I'm sure that $1200 must have set him back a bit. There sure are some beautiful people here. The signature book must have over 200 hundred names. Trouble is I don't know half of them. The other half I know or I'm related to in some way. We just didn't have the room in our schedules to get together. Too busy with life and all.
Yet, somehow, seems we all were able to make time on a day like today. I understand.

Well, everyone is sitting down in their seats, time for me to go back and lay down in mine. This gold platted detailing sure is nice, but oak wood would be just fine.

Snowflakes covered the page of the minister's Bible. Too many funerals this week, Pastor James committed the Scriptures to memory.   —

"Family and friends on this cold crisp December morning, we come to celebrate the life and memories of John Jackson, III. I know John would be so happy with you coming out on a day like today."

The Writing Hour

The Day passes his watch to the Night. The Moon trades places with the Sun. The house shifts to settle in for the evening. Hard wood floors creak under invisible feet. Egg-white walls groan with each pass of the night wind. Unlubricated door hinges herald the possible visit of peaceful spirits. The rise and fall of pre-recorded ocean waves set on continuous play, all serve as my nightly companions.

The cream background of acid-free unlined paper visible through a waterfall of disconnected words. Corner pieces of an incomplete jigsaw puzzle.

Finger-tip circular massages to the side of the head are feeble attempts to stem the flow of sentence possibilities. My hand is not quick enough. A traffic jam ensues. Thoughts collide in my mind too fast for me to capture the moments. Yet, three deep breaths and order is restored.

A one-click blue felt-tip pen becomes an extension of my hand. A chance to transform chaos into clarity. Where to begin? No northern star to guide my way. Once upon a time is taken by writers whose craft far exceeds my own. One dark night now shines by the light of the diamond stars. A land far away is brought close by the click of a mouse. The man in the moon brings no resolution nor a soft place to land.

Transformations occur with the roll of the pen. Light speed, my form of travel. Galaxies and distant worlds all gather at my fingertips. No past is sacred. No future is certain. Passions worthy of repentance are exposed. Reencountered memories too painful to forgive pounce from the fog.

Reciprocated love brings unmeasurable joy. Enemies are enticed to sample unimaginable peace. The umbrella of perceived protection is withdrawn, replaced by shackles of the truth. The mirror forgives imperfections. The measuring cup of beauty is shattered a victim to the ravages of time.

Time escapes. I have not the strength to try and recapture it. A sip of lukewarm water reinvigorates me. The pen resumes from each direction borrowing the bitter cold of the North, the complexities of the East, the generational traditions of the South, and the untamed expansion of the West.

The pen serenades with lyrics to tickle, tantalize, and tease the ears, bestowing unmerited favor. To others it offers a coordinated display of shame and reproach. The servant becomes too fearful to rule-frozen by the gift of freedom. But alas, forgiveness is only a sentence away.

Reversed lies become the truth. Hatred is rendered impotent unable to perform its dastardly deeds. Revenge is a dish discontinued from the menu. Pain a relic of a distant past. Lifelong fear, the first-cousin of doubt is overcome. Buried dreams rescued from the swift pull of quicksand. Owners of borrowed wisdom rejoice in their recent purchase. Hope is renewed. Faith is restored.

Yet, the battle of spirit and flesh rages on. The pen bound to its handler's will, chooses no sides. Words on the screen, ink to the paper, the orator's tongue, and missing lines in between will reveal the camouflaged truth. Elements of life are cocooned in a drop of rain.

Mercy is shared through a ray of sun. Grace is found in the gentleness of a whisper.

Rest is an unexperienced luxury. A story must be told. The traveler reaches the edge of the universe and still searches for more. Satisfaction a carrot dangling before his nose.

At last the dawn hovers above the horizon. Reserves of energy now depleted. The quiet drowns out the detectable heartbeat. Invisible creatures return to their sleep. The mystery of the caged bird's song revealed. The soul is not bound by mortal constraints. Mozart's work is complete. The symphony makes sense. A twelfth planet is found. Perhaps, another place to live.

Discontent gathers dust on a forgotten storage room museum shelf. Humankind is listening. Love abounds for all with more than enough to share.

The impossible becomes possible in the writing hour.

.

Brushing Mama's Hair

"Marvi? Is that you?"

"Yes, Mama."

"Girl, what are you doing home so early?" Mama asked. She was still groggy from the pain medicine. I checked her drip. Mama was using more medicine today. It was not a good day for her. The last thing she needed was to have to hear about my problems. "Oh, Mama I wasn't feeling well." *Which was true. I just punched a man. I was looking behind me. I was hoping that the police weren't following me. After all, Billy could have reported me to the police. It was well within his rights. I assaulted him in front of everybody. Oh my goodness, I saw the look of his face; on Faith's. What's wrong with me?*

"Hi Mama," I said gently kissing her forehead. Mama seemed smaller and smaller each day. That hospital bed in the middle of her room just seemed to consume her. "How are you feeling, Mama?"

"Oh, you know I'm just a little under the weather today, but I will be alright, baby. Mama's just a little tired."

"Mama, can I fix you something?"

"No, Marvi, I'm not too hungry right now, maybe later."

"Okay, Mama." I leaned to pick up the brush, sitting on top of her dresser. "Marvi, don't brush my hair today."

"Okay, Mama".

"Marvi sit with me 'til I go to sleep."

"Yes, Ma'am."

The nurse who sat with Mama during the day beckoned for me to step outside the room. The pump of medicine had quickly put Mama to sleep. "Marvi, I'm sorry to say this, but I truly think it's time for you to start making arrangements. I don't think your Mother is going to last out the week." No, I didn't want to hear what she was saying. Mama wasn't ready to go! I wasn't ready for Mama to go. What was I going to do without her!

"Get out!"

What!? The nurse looked at me with that well-trained look of understanding what I was feeling. She didn't understand anything! How dare she look at me like that.

"I said, get out of my house!" I was yelling now. "Lower your voice," the nurse said in a firm tone. Not once did she raise her voice but she let me know my behavior and tone was unacceptable. "Marvi, I understand what you are going through. But you have to think of your Mother now. We are keeping her comfortable. But it will be soon and you need to be ready. I can stay with her to-night if you need to take some time to prepare yourself. She is going to sleep through the night if anything chang-es I will let you know. You look like you need some rest. Marvi? Marvi? Did you hear what I just said?"

Of course I heard her. Did she think I was deaf? I hate the way she calls Mama, "Mother." She's Mama-my Mama. God is trying to take my Mama from me! But you can't have her! No! No! No! I won't let you have her! On top of that I have to listen to this stupid woman tell me that I need to prepare myself. How do you 'pre-pare' for God to take someone you love from you? Huh, Tell me! How?! That's what I wanted to say to her, but

21

instead I just acknowledged her truth. You know what you are right. It has been a long day and I'm tired. I am going to bed."

"Okay, Marvi, I just need to call the agency and let them know that I am staying the night."

"Fine. Do what you need to do. I'm going to bed." With one last look she turned to go downstairs to make her phone call.

I walked back into Mama's room. Somehow she had the hairbrush in her hand. "Mama? I thought you were asleep." Mama's eyes were wide open. "Marvi, come brush my hair."

"Yes, Ma'am." I slowly ran the brush through Mama's hair. I knew Mama was tired so I tried to be gentle. "Marvi, you can't fight God. We were born and then we die. All of us got to go through this journey. But what's special is what we do with what's in the middle. I ain't got much time Marvi. I'm thinking I'm not going to see tomorrow."

"Mama, No!"

"Yes, Marvi. I am tired. I'm too tired to keep holding on. I want to see Papa."

"No, Mama, No, Mama! I need you." "No Marvi, you're going to be alright. Just let that Boy love you. Watch out for his Daddy though. He got the "gift." Marvi?"

"Yes, Mama?"

"I love you." Then, it sounded like Mama was praying. Even in her last moment, she was giving homage to Him. Why Mama? Why? I don't know how long I sat brushing Mama's hair. "Marvi? Marvi?"

"I am brushing Mama's hair."

"Marvi?" The nurse came around to the bed and starting checking Mama's pulse, her breathing, and I don't know what else. I heard sirens and feet moving quickly. It all became a blur. I just wanted them to leave us alone. I needed to finish brushing Mama's hair.

The Suit in the Closet

Stripes with white background. A gift of a father's love. Cherished above all else. A relic of time. A reminder of a loving place. Covered in plastic to spare the ravages of time. Not to be worn, but remembered. Complemented by black "Stacy Adams" shoes, white buttoned down shirt, and satin lavender tie.

Simplicity. Complexity. Inexplicable emotion. Joy, sorrow, laughter, tears. Sacred.

The suit in the closet.

In the Middle of Somewhere

Two stop signs or three? Over the bridge, past Johnson's Creek, the fork in the road is still not in sight. A back wood dirt red road taken too far leads to a hidden bounty; miles of untouched, fourteen foot- high trees and fields plump for the harvesting. Land kissed by gold sunflowers, lilacs, and cattails swaying in the breeze.

The weight of an old grey, chipped paint house balances on five cement cinder blocks. I am greeted by "Beware of Dog" and "No Trespassing Signs" with a note of warning violators will be shot on sight. Over-sized flags wave high, symbols of one's ethnic pride. No welcomes here. Turn around I must. Within the time of two handshakes, I'm back to the road I started on. The air is thick with the smoke of burning brush.

Birds call to one another signaling my return. They bear witness to repeated attempts to find my destination. An over-enthusiastic GPS guide leads me to the edge of an embankment. The shrieks and clucks are reminiscent of laughter. Three large crows lead the chorus confident I can do nothing more than listen to their incessant chatter. Fortunately for them, my travels lead me elsewhere. Otherwise, I might be consuming crow tonight. I laugh at the irony of the thought. Crow meat is a meal best left uneaten.

Father, please help me find the way, a silent prayer offered to the Heavens above and to page 52 on the large red map catalog. My prayer is answered in the form of a three-tooth smile, trusting soul, sporting a farmer's tan, leather worn skin, denim overalls, and Elvis Presley sideburns.

Mesmerized by well-manicured side burns, through my nods of acknowledgement I fail to keep count of the down-the road, past the stop sign, left-right turns to make. The stranger disappears into rows of seven-foot-high stalks of corn just as quickly as he appeared.

Two stop signs or three, I cannot recall. I stay on my current path, moving forward. Around the bin, fresh rolled bales of hay, goats, range-free chickens, and cows content their scheduled visit to the stockades is not today.

Another forty-four miles give way to horizontal land-
scapes untouched by human hands. The skilled strokes
of a grand painter cover the canvas of a morning sky with
hues of red, pink, and hazel, accolades given by the howls
of a pack of wolves. A masterful sculptor designed majestic mountains to stand guard over foam-white turbu-
lent rivers.

Another hundred miles bring towns with unpronouncea-
ble names, whose mix-matched vowels signify some
significant historical origin. A mispronunciation, a tell-
tale sign of an unknowledgeable tourist. But the traveler
must reach her destination by some self-imposed dead-
line.

Thus I continue on, bombarded by every other highway
sign proclamations of food, gas, lodging, pickled eggs,
and homemade beef jerky, hints to what lies ahead. All
escapes from back-sweat inducing heat.

Population and elevation welcome me to indicate how
high above sea level to meet new people. No time for
that perhaps on the next visit, I'll exit the highway to say
"Hi". But for now smog-free, single digit temperatures,

allow me a reprieve from man-made air, interrupted only by a pungent whiff of recent road- kill carcasses.

Peace and tranquility are exchanged for six lanes of race-car drivers, willfully ignorant of decorative, sporadically placed speed limit signs. Honks and descriptive hand gestures indicate their discomfort at having to share the road with someone other than themselves.

A dance of bob and weave plays out before me. A premonition fulfilled. Turns taken too fast mix with roads too slick. Yellow carp now covers flesh mingled with steel. Home by dinnertime is no longer an option. Missed opportunities to say "I love you", not recaptured.

A lifetime of memories replaced by a single white cross adorned with red, white, and blue flowers, teddy bears, and silver balloons, marked the side of the road. Now this somewhere town is five members less.

Two hundred miles later, bright city lights waken the tranquil mind. Massive phallic structures ascend high to the sky, a combination of over-indulged egos and engineering brilliance.

A light mist begins to fall. The over-hanging dark clouds empty their contents. Windshield wiper blades on high become like plastic knives stabbing the ocean, useless.

Incapable of fighting Mother Nature, with what wisdom remains, weary from the road I find rest in an unfamiliar bed, with medium stuffed pillows, and 11am checkouts.

Tomorrow will begin again in the middle of somewhere.

Words

I possess commutative, associative, and distributive relationships with words. Juxtaposed phrases freeze the Bully in his tracks. Unable to comprehend or process my true intent he finds no pleasure in today's scheduled torment.

Words spared me from the onslaught of demeaning actions.

Intricate parallel and perpendicular phrases catapult me above the status of a pig-tailed girl wearing a tattered well-worn dress.

Words rescue me from outward adorning and trappings which serve as clever disguises from inward torrential storms.

Perfect intonation, phonics, and dictation distinguish me from the complacent crowd and suggest that in fact my words contribute meaning to a deeper conversation.

The Left Side of the Bed

Feeble attempt to hide the truth only reveal it more. Cast down eyes expose secret guilt. Our undefiled bed is now a resting place for two known strangers. No more meetings in the middle. We cower with unease on respective sides of the bed. Gone are gentle caresses and abandon passion. Now only barricades of pillows are cleverly constructed between us. Insincere excuses of tired and stressed seem devoid of planning.

Flashes of lightning evident through creases in custom designed shades reveal the storm without, perhaps a mirror of the turbulence within. Our bed serves as a place to rest from the days' events and to ponder unspoken thoughts. Desired fantasies once whispered in receptive feminine ears, are replaced by restless snores and sleep-spoken transgressions in the night.

Truth and hopes for the future flow like fresh water from a new form spring. Now, no words exchanged. Silence covers like a warm fleece blanket. Assumed good nights and a presupposed "I love you'" are the night ritual.

Someone took my place. Her name is not important. Besides, you would never tell. Your gentleman's honor to spare me some "unforeseen" shame prevents your revelation of the truth. A soul tormented by voices of the past. But I know.

Broad shoulders are burdened down by the weight of undisclosed transgressions. Bright and shiny eyes now stale and dull from misplaced trust. Lips once plump, soft and moist from God united love are now thin, cracked, and dry from adulterous kisses.

You toss and turn; rest eludes you as guilt wraps around you in 600 count thread sheets. A blue led light clock, your counter to the next days beginning. No comfort provided.

Consummated solace in a stranger's arm only widens the black hole you desire to fill. Her promises of fulfilling love now become like unpaid debts. Your loins long and strong now limp from the bankrupt love of her wicked arms. Her phantom mask is removed. The acid of her lies leave you shivering and burnt. A mistake soon realized.

Home becomes your bed of choice. Thus, promises made, you seek to renew. A faithful heart broken by immoral deeds, you desire to heal. An ignored flame, you wish to rekindle.

The realization of soul healing comfort lies within your grasp next to you on the left side of the bed. I am yours, more precious than gold and silver. The undigested cold dish of well-deserved revenge is too bitter for my palate. Instead, I choose the rightful warmth of complete forgiveness.

Yet, unrepentant pride blocks your path. Paranoid fear of uncertain responses hinders your actions. Your dread grows for no need. What you try to shield is apparent. Although words are not said, I know.

The Path I Walk

Cinderella's slippers break beneath the weight of imperfection. Blood flows from slivers embedded in my flesh. The path I walk requires a sturdier pair.

I trudge forward. Imperfection is my reflection. Desire for soul's eternal peace is the torch which lights my way. Misguided notions, well-intentioned plans divert me from my goal. Unearned grace leads me back.

I continue to trudge on; clouds of thoughts shielded from mortal games by the canopy of truth. A cocooned mind is transported from ailments which seek to strip the body of healing power.

Whispered wicked words are foiled attempts to disqualify me from life's race. Voices taunt me desiring to steal my strength. Devious efforts to still my soul go unheeded. Well warned of their plots, I maneuver outside their grasp. Lost ways restored; forgotten past remembered.

Joy dances with pain. Happiness converses with sorrow. Rejoice, for pain knows no prejudice. Sorrow is blind to the color of skin. Equal is the distance I travel. Unjust is the road I take.

Minus a sturdier pair of slippers my obstacles still remain but finish this race I must! The trophy within arms' distance seems miles away. I stumble into the ditch of unfulfilled, well-intentioned deeds. The finish jumps from the tips of my fingertips moving further from my view.

Alas! A phantom strength pokes me from behind forcing me to carry on. Mercy and love build an invisible hand to pull me out. They wrap around my feet. The Master's silent voice calls me by name encouraging me to rise and continue. Finally, the perfect pair are mine to wear. Thus, I begin again along the path I walk.

Once Upon a Time

Once upon a time I believed you. Now, this sleeping beauty is awake to the truth of the big bad wolf.

You huff and you puff but my house still stands. Even as you sneak and slink in shadows, the light reveals your inner most thoughts. You possess what you do not want and seek for what you can't have. It runs from you in fear. Your outstretched hand is a scam. Your voice a shrill noise to tender ears. You are a masquerade.

The roses at your feet are like prickly cactus. The fairytale ends and the truth begins. You are not what you seem. You are eroded. Pomp and circumstance removed like the bashing of the waves against hot summer sand.

Mine

10,000 words are a whisper. 4-inch novels are only a drop. How do I express my gratitude? How do I show my love? All cleverly composed, yet still fall short. Picasso's painting and Beethoven's composition are perfectly intertwined, yet still pale by comparison.

When all that I have is never enough. I give anyway. When all that I could say seems nonsense and jibberish. I still speak. When all that I do is infinitely minute. I still love. When all that I could hope for comes to fruition. I still believe.

When all the thoughts of mind, body, and soul converge together, none come close to this moment. You with your perfect fingers and toes covered in black ink, pressed to mark your feet to a page. Straight black hair and uncommon blue eyes. Oh, what a blessing this child called mine.

What Others Say

Either you guide me or you hinder me; no space exists between. Pay no mind to what others say. Bitter words fueled by inward caverns filled with deadly ash. Volcano spewed content masks well disguised fear.

No skill of the surgeon's blade can replicate God-given beauty. I am a canvas blended by golds, browns, reds, blues and grays. Light and dark. Silence and sound.

Ignorance overflows with no place for the truth. To lie in sorrow and complain of unfair treatment leads to empty places. Strength lies in bold recognition of joy no man can tame. Boulders of ice are no match for unbridled heat.

Yes, you yell and scream but your voice remains small. As for me, I rise and stand tall.

Empty is the space beneath your skin. Too heavy is your sin for you to cast the first stone. You desire to shorten my stride and find comfort with my absence from view.

My courage in spite of your childlike attempts angers you more.

I pay no mind to what others say. They bring not the rain, wind and snow. Their only power is what I have given to them through faithless fear. I take it back now without warning. You're unprepared. Beneath the soles of your feet I no longer choose to stay. Instead, beside you with cadence as equal with head held high, I walk.

Oh, I pay no mind to what others say. My place is no longer at the back but seated at the front. I emerge from the shadows renewed with focus and purpose.

My victory is shared with those who pay no mind to what others say. Phantom fear once made real by the power I gave you, I now reclaim. The key to freedom slips from your pocket too quickly for you to recapture. You stand on the sidelines; an observer to the destruction you set in motion. Now stalled by the grace of God and His mercy bestowed.

To admit you are wrong does not resonate. To believe that we are right is incomprehensible. To share knowledge and sacred truths overwhelms you. But alas, I pay no mind to what others say.

Grandma Faces Forward

Life lessons learned too young remain branded on the mind. A doctor's office waiting room exposes a child to hate in the form of a human wearing a starched white shirt, black suspenders, and blue flannel pants.

Grandma is a tree that will not be moved-prepared for battle armed with strength and courage beyond your ability to understand. You try to flank her from the side; intimidate from behind. But Grandma yields her authority to a higher power. You try to break her spirit with the stones of evil hateful words hurled her way, but you have no power. Grandma faces forward.

Grandma's smile spreads slowly then smoothly throughout her face. She hides a secret you want to know. But your heart is hardened by ignorance and disdain. You and your wicked masters before you held the keys to the chains. But Grandma uses knowledge applied to consume both key and chain.

Your rage is evident by the clenched fists and red flush pressed against sun leathered skin and peppered grey hair. Your words echo louder against calm white walls.

Your disbelief grows as your insults bounce ineffectively against the protective shield around Grandma and me.

As a tigress defending her cub, I would love to pounce and tear you from limb to limb. But God has mercy even for you. My anger too soon subsides.

I find comfort and peace in that whatever this force may be, it protects me from you. Perhaps it is the soul force full of faith, combined with the power of works. But for me, you were defeated because Grandma faces forward.

I am calmed and soothed by the well-timed opening of the doctor's office door. I am blessed by the return to quiet as your mouth quickly closes. You cower and wither away, silenced by the presence of the alpha male with smooth mocha skin and snow-capped hair. Grandma faces forward, but Grandpa faces you.

This Author, Her Name

What to tell, what to keep.

Do I give away all and just rewards reap?

Or do misconstrued meanings attached to innocent words bring regret and weeping?

Can trust be built behind a make-believe screen where recipients of my thoughts, hopes, and dreams remain unseen?

Do they know within the click of their gadgets,

I am dismissed perhaps possibly accepted?

Do they care or is this just a game?

Never knowing, never caring for this author, her name.

Travel Home Softly

Travel home softly. Let the wind not find you. Leave no trace of footsteps. Hide behind the mist. Travel as quickly as the water flows through the pine and thicket. Move quickly as the spoken whisper, silently as the morning dew, gentle as the falling rain.

Move slowly to gentle peace. Make haste to anger's release.

Move with the strength of light, yet shielded by the cover of night.

Let neither right hand nor left know the other's will, lest it masters the other's skill; stay to your journey, no deterrent from your focus. Through dread of tired eyes, hold fast! Soon comes the sunrise.

Majestic reds tickle passionate blues; still more miles till I'm through. Reserve your will, energy, and might to battle through the desert's heat. Intensity scorches but does not kill, eagerly sapping the master's will.

Note each moment, remember them all, each precious by name them call. Honeysuckle, lavender, and green, all images of God's perfect scheme.

A canvas layered by colors both pale and dark, a tapestry woven to mimic the heart. Only so many more miles to go; just one more bin, one more curve, one more state line. Almost there. Soon to be in the arms of him who cares.

A Mother's Prayer

In the blink of an eye, a lifetime has passed. In the span of a breadth, one comes to an end.

In the absence of my presence, fill their hearts with peace and compassion.

Replace tears with joy and laughter. Confusion with trust. Doubt with faith.

Lord, keep them safe. Let trouble pass over their way.

Let them be invisible to those who seek to do them harm.

Let your Mercy and Grace be the coolness of the pillow to soothe their tired heads.

Let understanding and wisdom be the blanket to keep them warm and safe against the bitter cold of a torn and divided world.

In the midst of the storm, let them hold to you, their anchor;

In the brightness of the sunshine, let your love be the smile that lights their way;

Let your Word be the shield to protect them, guard them from foolish and ill - advised paths.

Let those who see them, see you.

No Room

I have no room.

I have no room for fear. It takes up space designated for higher goals. I have no room for ignorance and stupidity which scars the face with deep unrecognizable grooves. It clouds the mind with falseness and causes unnatural aging of the soul. I have no room for hate with its shards of glass and cobblestones. It deters me from the path to salvation. I have no room for those who choose to destroy with their words and actions. I have no room for misery enhanced by the company it chooses to keep. I have no room to give in or to give up.

I have no room.

The Wind

The wind blows to move stagnation. The wind howls to herald its coming. The wind grows and unites to unleash its anger on all that lies in its path. The wind plays with the leaves and reveals its heart. The wind changes so not to stay in one place too long. The wind calls no place home yet lives everywhere. The wind is energy, unbound, abiding by and answering only to the laws of nature.

The wind's arms bring a gift from afar. Its messages carried from the tip of the top and from the top of the bottom. The wind is gentle, brushing feather-like kisses on unsuspecting cheeks.

The wind is playful sending whispers across the waves of water.

The wind is life, complex, unpredictable, whole, and complete. It travels the air, across land and sea, through darkness and light. The wind is a brisk cold morning or a hot stinging afternoon breeze.

The wind's breath is gentle, strong, and destructive; it is both sweet, like the gentle brush against the check and pungent like the scalding heat on a steamy hot summer's day.

The wind is objective. It responds to perfect conditions. The wind has no prejudices and is not partial to regional demands. The wind moves the man of conscious and the man of confusion.

The wind harbors no notion of right or wrong. The wind shows power but extends mercy.

In moments, the wind is quiet. Other times, loud and boisterous.

All peoples, great or small, rich or poor, are recipients of its grace and its formidable power.

I welcome its embrace.

The wind brings me to my knees with minimal effort.

With its breath, the wind compels me to remove my protective layers to reveal the me underneath.

The wind calls to me without knowing my name; words spoken without speaking.

Jacquinita A. Rose

About the Author

Jacquinita Rose's major influences in literature are Robert Frost, Virginia Wolfe and Maya Angelou. This can be seen in much of the imagery and poetic style of certain stories such as *I Hide in the Rain* and *What Others Say.* Rose has been writing since she was a little girl and writing continues to be her release for self-expression. Much of her writings are also inspired by her grandparents, her children, and every day happenings around her. Rose will write until the pencil breaks. Even then, she'll find another and keep writing!

Other Jacquinita A. Rose Titles

Shhh, Grown Folks Is Talking

The Road Taken (Her Heart Heals Quietly Book 1)

When Dreams Finally Come (Her Heart Heals Quietly Book 2)

Stained Glass Windows (Her Heart Heals Quietly Book 3)

Faith Has Conquered Fear

Previously Published Short Stories

The Right Side of Happy

A Day Like Today

In The Middle of Somewhere

The Writing Hour

Brushing Mama's Hair